School Bus Saves the Day

Peter Bently

Illustrated by Louise Conway

School Bus arrives on time to take the class to the **city carnival**.

Bus Driver turns on the **warning lights** and raises the **stop sign**. The children **board** the bus.

Mr Hodges, the teacher, checks the register.
"Where's Harry?" he asks.

"Here I am, Sir!" pants Harry.
"I left my lunch box in class!"

When everyone is aboard, Bus Driver closes the **doors** and **starts** the **engine**.

vroom!

Bus Driver turns off the **warning lights**, lowers the **stop sign** and heads for the city.

Mr Hodges speaks into the **intercom**.
"First we will see a few sights, then
we will watch the **carnival parade**."

"We're passing the **ZOO**," says Holly.
"I can see the **elephants!**"

School Bus **drives** into the **city centre**.

They pass the **river** and Mr Hodges points out all the **sights**.

School Bus stops at the **park** so the
class can have their **picnic**.

It is a hot and sunny day,
so the children sit in the shade.

After the picnic, School Bus heads for the **main avenue**.

But a **police car** stops the bus...

From School Bus's **big windows** the children
have a great view of the parade.

SPIKEWOOD SCHOOL

There are **marching bands**,
dancers, acrobats and **jugglers.**

There are all kinds
of colourful **carnival floats.**

"**Wow!**" says Harry. "Those **stiltwalkers**
are as tall as School Bus!"

"Where are the carnival king and queen?" exclaims Mr Hodges.

"There they are!" says Bus Driver.
"But why isn't their float moving?
I'll go and find out."

"The **truck** that pulls our **float** has **broken down**," explains the carnival queen.

"We'll miss the parade!"
cries the carnival king.

"I have an idea!" says Bus Driver.
"Don't worry, we'll soon get the parade moving!"

The **police officer** holds back the crowds as Bus Driver **reverses** School Bus to the broken-down truck.

Bus Driver **unhitches** the float from the truck and **fixes** it to School Bus's **towbar**.

"Hooray!" cheers the carnival queen. "Now we can **go!**"

"Not just yet," smiles Mr Hodges.

"Come on class, let's get all the **decorations** off the truck!"

The parade starts up again.
The crowd cheer in delight when
they see **School Bus.**

School Bus is brightly decorated, with all its **lights** flashing. Everyone agrees it is the **biggest** and **best** float of all.

"Hooray for School Bus!" cry the carnival king and queen. "You saved the parade!"

Let's look at
School Bus

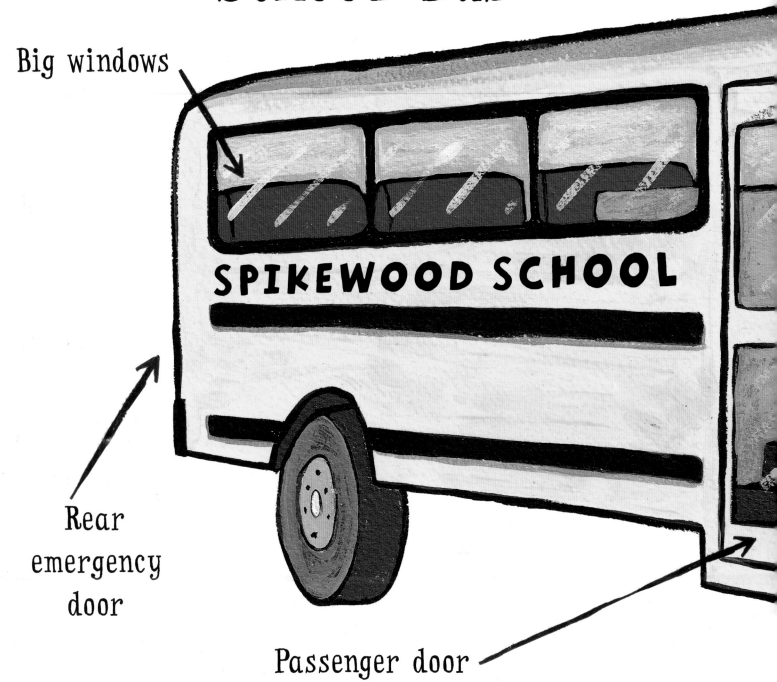

Big windows

SPIKEWOOD SCHOOL

Rear
emergency
door

Passenger door

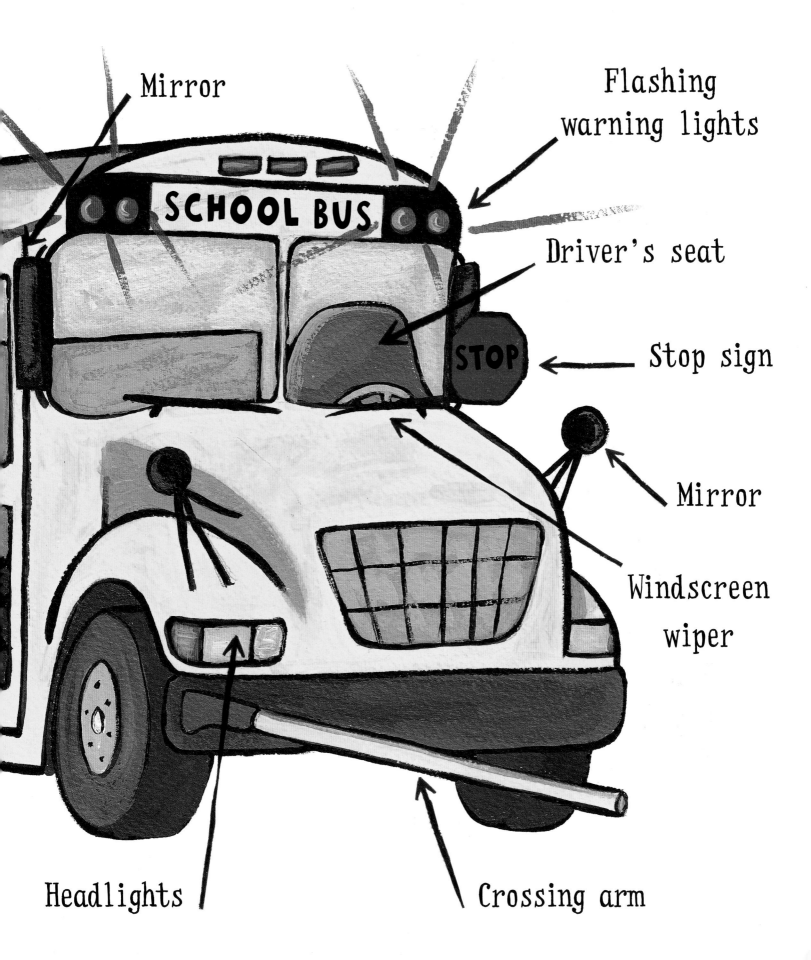

Mirror

Flashing warning lights

SCHOOL BUS

Driver's seat

STOP

Stop sign

Mirror

Windscreen wiper

Headlights

Crossing arm

Other Types of Bus:

Minibus

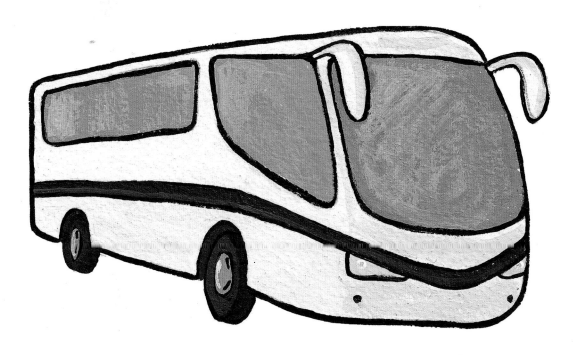

Long-distance coach

Public bus

Open-top sightseeing bus

For St Michael's CE
Primary School, Oxford P.B.

For my children,
Kieran & Tabitha L.C.

Designer: Verity Clark
Art Director: Laura Roberts-Jensen
Editors: Tasha Percy and Sophie Hallam
Editorial Director: Vicky Garrard

First published in the UK in 2016 by
QED Publishing
Part of The Quarto Group
The Old Brewery, 6 Blundell Street
London, N7 9BH

www.qed-publishing.co.uk

A catalogue record for this book is available from the British Library.

ISBN 978 1 78493 116 2

Printed in China